SPORTS GREAT KOBE BRYANT

—Sports Great Books—

SPORTS GREAT
KOBE BRYANT

Glen Macnow

—Sports Great Books—

Enslow Publishers, Inc.

40 Industrial Road   PO Box 38
Box 398   Aldershot
Berkeley Heights, NJ 07922   Hants GU12 6BP
USA   UK
http://www.enslow.com

Dedicated to Lois Stone, who could write ten books on hard work and the love of family.

Library of Congress Cataloging-in-Publication Data

Macnow, Glen.
    Sports great Kobe Bryant / Glen Macnow.
       p. cm. — (Sports great books)
    Includes index.
    Summary: Describes the life and career of the Los Angeles Lakers basketball star Kobe Bryant.
    ISBN 0-7660-1264-6
    1. Bryant, Kobe, 1978– Juvenile literature. 2. Basketball players—United States Biography Juvenile literature. 3. Los Angeles Lakers (Basketball team) Juvenile literature. [1. Bryant, Kobe, 1978– . 2. Basketball players. 3. Afro-Americans Biography.] I. Title. II. Title: Kobe Bryant. III. Series.
GV884.B794M33 2000
796.323'092—dc21
[B]
                        99-15908
                        CIP

Printed in the United States of America

10 9 8 7 6 5 4 3 2 1

To Our Readers:
All Internet addresses in this book were active and appropriate when we went to press. Any comments or suggestions can be sent by e-mail to Comments@enslow.com or to the address on the back cover.

Illustration Credits: Andrew D. Bernstein/NBA Photos, pp. 9, 11, 17, 23, 32, 39, 48, 50, 54; Andy Hayt/NBA Photos, p. 57; Fernando Medina/NBA Photos, p. 41; Glenn James/NBA Photos, pp. 21, 36, 45, 59; Nathaniel S. Butler/NBA Photos, pp. 14, 26, 30.

Cover Illustration: Andrew D. Bernstein/NBA Photos.

Contents

Chapter 1

He was just eighteen when he joined the National Basketball Association (NBA). That was not long after he took a Hollywood starlet to his senior prom. He drives a BMW and wears a silly, floppy hat he bought in a secondhand store. He calls his father, "Sir," and reads books such as *Moby Dick* on his own time, by his own choice.

Kobe Bryant is not like most people. He is certainly not like most NBA players. And that is why he may just be pro basketball's future.

He was raised in Italy—a tall, African-American kid who stuck to hoops while the other kids there played soccer. When he was just eight, a cousin called him from the United States and started raving about some human highlight film he had seen on television.

"You won't believe this," his cousin said.

"Believe what?"

"Believe Air."

"Air," of course, was Michael Jordan. The cousin sent videotape, and Kobe Bryant watched number twenty-three wag his tongue and soar through the air. Some day, Kobe decided, he would do that, too. He began collecting other videos. He took a liking to Magic Johnson, the great point guard, and began wearing a Los Angeles Lakers jacket around Italy. He studied the spin moves of Earl "The Pearl" Monroe and the tricks of Pistol Pete Maravich.

Kobe Bryant learned to respect history. Through hard work, Kobe became the best twelve-year-old basketball player anyone had ever seen. And then the best fourteen-year-old player. And then the best sixteen-year-old player, starring for Lower Merion High School, outside Philadelphia.

By then, dozens of colleges made it known they wanted Kobe to lead them to an NCAA title. He scored 1,100 on his SATs (college entrance exams). He could have gone to nearly any school and gotten As. But he decided to do something that only a handful have tried, and fewer have succeeded at. He decided, at age eighteen, to turn professional.

Less than two years later, Bryant was starring in the NBA All-Star Game. His favorite team from childhood—the Los Angeles Lakers—cruised to the NBA Western Conference Finals with Bryant featured as the sixth man, or the first substitute off the bench.

What an amazing ride it has been for this young man.

"When I look at how fast and how well things have gone, I just have to pinch myself," he said. "Then I look ahead to my future and I think things can get even better. But I can't get caught up in all of the hype or I could crash."

The future? Many basketball fans look at the future and see a picture of Kobe Bryant. They see very little chance of him crashing.

The NBA has been built on personalities. In the 1980s, the great rivalry between Magic Johnson of the Lakers and Larry Bird of the Boston Celtics brought about terrific television

Soaring through the air, Kobe Bryant is about to throw down a slam dunk. When he was a kid, Bryant used to watch highlight films of Michael Jordan, possibly the greatest dunker of them all.

ratings. In the 1990s, Michael Jordan skied his way to six championships, ten scoring titles, and five Most Valuable Player awards. But when the Jordan era ended just before the new century began, the question was, who would succeed Jordan? Who would be the new face of the NBA?

Bryant's Lakers teammate Shaquille O'Neal seemed a candidate, but he did not have the magic. Grant Hill and Penny Hardaway are excellent players, but neither seems to be quite the superstar needed for the job.

So who is the next great hope? After Jordan's retirement following the 1997–98 season, that question was still not answered. But do not count out a six-foot seven-inch string bean who speaks two languages and has no tattoos and no earrings.

"I've never seen anyone like him," said Lakers teammate Robert Horry. "For example, I've never seen somebody who can watch a move that another guy does and learn it as quickly as he does. Usually it takes so long to get a move down, to learn the footwork. Sometimes it takes all summer. But he'll work on it, and two days later you'll see it in his game. Amazing."

Kobe Bryant's unquenchable desire to study and to learn may be what separates him from the pack. Consider this two-game episode from January 1998, during his second season:

Against the Phoenix Suns on January 21, Bryant poured in a team-high 25 points and snared 5 rebounds. His best work that night came from the outside, where he made three of four three-point attempts. Bryant's long-range jumper arches high in the air. Sometimes it looks as if it will hit the arena ceiling. It gently falls back to the court, usually passing through the net with a gentle "swish."

That night against the Suns, however, Bryant noticed someone else's shot. He studied Rex Chapman, Phoenix's veteran guard. Chapman would streak down the court, fake a pass, and then stop suddenly to pull up for a jumper while

During a game that took place on January 21, 1998, Kobe Bryant burned the Suns for 25 points.

other players ran by him. Watching Chapman's move, Bryant said it reminded him of a cartoon, in which the Roadrunner stops on a dime, while his enemy—Wile E. Coyote—continues to run off the edge of a cliff.

Bryant knew he had to have that move.

So for the next week, while the Lakers traveled on the road, Bryant spent all his spare time in the gym. He practiced running and then stopping as quickly as he could. First he tried it without the ball. Then, when he had that down, he spent hours more working on the move while dribbling. Only after he had perfected that did he try finishing the move by shooting the ball. In all, he probably spent twenty hours that week, mostly by himself, trying to get down one single move.

The Lakers traveled to New Jersey to take on the Nets on January 28. Bryant came off the bench six minutes into the game. He immediately had a hot hand. He took a bounce pass from teammate Eddie Jones and cut toward the basket. But Nets forward Kerry Kittles blocked his way. Bryant neatly shifted the ball from his right hand to his left. The move froze Kittles, allowing Bryant to throw up a nifty left-handed underhand two pointer.

This was one of Kobe Bryant's best games of the season. He scored 26 points and pulled down 5 rebounds. His lightning-quick moves caused Nets defender Sam Cassell to foul him so often that Cassell was sent to the bench. But Bryant's greatest move came late in the game.

He grabbed a high-arching rebound near his own basket and quickly started down court on a fast break. Nets guard Kendall Gill—an excellent defender—sprinted to catch up with him. Just as Bryant reached the top of the key he stopped. But Gill could not stop. As Gill kept running, nearly into the front row of seats, Bryant pulled up and hit a soft three pointer. It was just like what Rex Chapman had done to the Lakers a week earlier. The move brought a standing ovation—not from the Nets' hometown fans, but from Bryant's teammates. They knew how hard he had worked to master the move.

Hard work, it seems, is Kobe Bryant's answer for most challenges. That, and belief in himself. Those are good life lessons for any young person. Late in the 1997–98 season, Bryant went into the first slump of his career. Over a four-game period he made just 12 of the 47 shots he attempted. That is a 26 percent success rate, which is terrible by NBA standards. Bryant called it the worst he had played since his second year of high school.

"This is the toughest stretch I've ever gone through. I'm hating it," he said after a game in which he heard a few fans booing him. "But I'm also still loving it. It's part of the challenge. That's part of the fun. Am I pressing? Maybe. That's something I'll have to think about. I want to go through periods when I'm struggling, because that's when you learn. And the more you learn, the better you get."

The next night he went out and scored 25 points in a win over the San Antonio Spurs.

Kobe Bryant's talent and work ethic have taken him far at an early age. While still a teenager, he owned a mansion in the Los Angeles suburb of Pacific Palisades. He owns several fancy cars, and more nice clothes than he can ever wear. Many companies have offered to pay him well to do commercials for their products. It is not just the basketball star that advertisers want to show off. It is the total person.

"His smile lights up a room," said John Hollowell, director of marketing for Adidas, whose shoes Bryant wears on the court. "And Kobe is a good person with family values. We like it that Joe and Pam [Kobe's parents] are always there with him."

Joe and Pam Bryant are almost certainly the only parents of an NBA star who live with their child. They share the

When people talk about Kobe Bryant, they often mention his good character. Here a determined Bryant takes the ball away from an opposing player.

Los Angeles home with Kobe and, sometimes, his two older sisters.

NBA's up-and-coming superstar has a solid home life with his family. He has all the toys a young man could ask for, but he also has a solid value system that keeps him from getting carried away with those toys. Bryant has a great job as the first man off the bench for the Los Angeles Lakers and a work ethic that drives him to be the best he can be.

Perhaps ten years from now, Kobe Bryant will reach the lofty heights of all-time greats such as Michael Jordan and Magic Johnson. Someday, perhaps, his number eight jersey will be retired by the Lakers. Many experts predict he will also be inducted into the Basketball Hall of Fame.

For now, Kobe Bryant is just enjoying the journey. Having fun is an important part of life. Bryant's parents taught him that lesson, too.

Chapter 2

To understand Kobe Bryant, you must first know his parents. They are the two people who taught him about life on and off the court. They gave him his work ethic, his talent, his intelligence, and even his flashiness. Today, the bond between son and parents is strong. You can see it in the way Kobe touches his father's hand as they sit side by side and talk, or the way he hugs his mother with gusto in public.

Joe Bryant, Kobe's dad, was a Philadelphia basketball legend. As a teenager, he was known as Jumping Bean. The nickname eventually changed to Jelly Bean. Joe Bryant became a star player at LaSalle University in North Philadelphia in the 1970s. He was a six-foot nine-inch forward who could dribble like a guard.

Joe Bryant grew up in a strong, solid family. One Saturday, when he was a teenager, Joe went to visit his grandparents in Center City, Philadelphia. Sitting on the porch, he spotted a teenage girl who happened to be visiting her grandparents at the same time. "I think I'm going to marry her," Joe thought to himself.

When Kobe's father, Joe Bryant, was in college, he was known as a big man who could dribble like a guard. It seems as if those skills have been passed down to his son.

The girl's name was Pam Cox. She was a smart and studious girl, as well as a fine athlete. Her brother, John "Chubby" Cox, turned out to be a basketball star who competed against Joe Bryant in college and later played a season in the NBA. Chubby Cox introduced the two teenagers, who quickly fell in love and eventually married.

Joe Bryant was LaSalle's top player for three seasons. He left school to turn pro after his junior year because his family needed the money. The Golden State Warriors made him their first pick of the 1975 college draft. But Bryant and the Warriors could not agree on a contract, so they traded him to his hometown team, the Philadelphia 76ers.

In the NBA, Joe Bryant became a defensive specialist. He was never a star, but he was a valuable member of the 1976–77 Sixers squad that went to the NBA Finals before losing to Bill Walton and the Portland Trail Blazers. Mostly, his job was to spell (give a break to) the 76ers starting forwards, Julius Erving and George McGinnis.

Joe and Pam had two daughters, Shaya and Sharia. Then, in 1978, Pam Bryant gave birth to a son. They named him Kobe in honor of their favorite Japanese steak house in the Philadelphia suburb of King of Prussia. Kobe is a type of beef found on the menu at most Japanese restaurants.

From the start, the little boy loved basketball. When he was three years old, Kobe would tune the living room television to his father's game. He would set up a Nerf ball hoop in front of the television set and imitate his dad from start to finish. He would toss the little ball into the basket, rest between quarters, and even sip from his own water bottle on the floor. When his dad toweled off on television, Kobe would grab his own towel and wipe down.

"He'd say, 'Mom, feel my neck, I'm sweating,'" recalls

Pam Bryant. "He was always imitating his dad. And he'd tell me, even then: 'Mom, I'm going to play in the NBA.'"

In 1984, when Kobe was six, his father's NBA career ended with the Houston Rockets. Joe Bryant thought about going into coaching, but decided instead to take his game to Europe. He and Pam and the three kids moved to Rieti, Italy, so Joe could play pro basketball there. It was the start of a family adventure that lasted eight years. During that time, the Bryants moved from town to town in Italy. Kobe learned things about life and basketball that he would have never learned in the United States.

The first thing he learned as a first grader was that very few Italian children played his favorite sport.

"After school, I would be the only guy on the basketball court, working on my moves, and then kids would start showing up with their soccer ball," Kobe said. "I could hold them off if there were two or three of them. But when they got to be eleven or twelve, I had to give up the court. It was either go home or be the goalkeeper."

Because Kobe and his two older sisters were just learning to speak Italian, they had to work harder than most other students. But they quickly fell in love with their new home. The food was great. The streets were safe. And in Italian culture, children and parents were very close in most households. The Bryants—like native Italians—would gather for a big family dinner and then sit at the table, eating and talking for hours.

While few Italian children played basketball, the country was full of big-time basketball fans. They would carry team flags, wave scarves, and wear their team colors to every game. At packed arenas, fans would throw coins at visiting players. They would chant and sing and hop in place for entire games. Joe Bryant—a defensive-minded player in the NBA—became a scoring star, averaging 20 points per game. The Italian fans loved him. They even wrote a song about him that went, "You know the player who's better than Magic [Johnson] or [Kareem-Abdul] Jabbar? It's Joseph, Joseph Bryant."

After school each day, Kobe would bike to his father's team practice. While the players worked out, Kobe shot baskets in the corner. Sometimes he would go one-on-one against the professionals. By age ten, he was sometimes beating them. By age twelve, he would occasionally put on a shooting display for fans during halftime of his dad's games. Kobe always got a standing ovation.

Every few days, the mail would come with videotapes from across the Atlantic Ocean. Kobe's grandparents sent tapes of American television shows and movies. Before Kobe and his sisters could watch anything, it had to be reviewed by their parents. Movies with violence or nudity were not allowed. "Growing up, it was all 'Babes in Toyland' and 'Willie Wonka and the Chocolate Factory,'" Kobe recalled. "Those are things kids should be exposed to. You don't need to see all this violence."

His favorite videotapes, of course, were of NBA basketball games, and his favorite team became the Los Angeles Lakers. Kobe wore a gold-and-purple leather Lakers jacket even on the hottest days. His bedroom walls were covered with posters of Magic Johnson. The Lakers played six thousand miles away, but to Kobe, they were the home team. He watched tapes of their games over and over again, as someone would watch a favorite movie. He memorized big plays. He replayed highlights, backward and forward, in regular speed and slow motion.

Joe Bryant watched too, right next to his son. Joe would explain to Kobe why some moves worked and others did not. He would have Kobe study what players did with their shoulders, their feet, their heads. As far as Kobe knew, he was just

Growing up, Kobe Bryant's favorite team was the Los Angeles Lakers. It is fitting that he would eventually don a Lakers uniform.

getting to understand his heroes a little better. But then he would go outside and imitate the world's greatest players in his own backyard.

Today, Kobe Bryant will tell you that his fallaway shot was inspired by Hakeem Olajuwon and his jump shot by Oscar Robertson. From Earl "The Pearl" Monroe, he learned how to fake one way and then go another. From Pistol Pete Maravich, he learned the little tricks that drive an opponent crazy. If, indeed, Kobe Bryant turns out to be basketball's future, one of the nicest things about him is that he appreciates its past.

There were not many kids for Kobe to play against in Italy, so he learned by practicing with his father's teammates. And almost every day, there was a one-on-one game pitting father against son. "I didn't beat him in any of those games until I was sixteen," Kobe said. "Dad was real physical with me. When I was fourteen or fifteen he started cheating. He'd elbow me in the mouth, rip my lip open. Then my mother would walk out on the court, and the elbows would stop." Looking back, Kobe said the nasty play made him tougher.

By 1991, the Italian League team Joe Bryant played for was in financial trouble. (In 1999, Kobe Bryant himself bought 50 percent of the team.) In addition, the three Bryant children were now teenagers. Joe and Pam wanted to prepare their children for college in the United States. So they moved back to the Philadelphia suburbs, where Joe Bryant took a job as assistant coach at his old school, LaSalle University.

After seven years in Europe, Kobe felt some culture shock back in the United States. To make things easier, his parents gave him a crash course in American culture. He watched videos of *The Cosby Show*, listened to Janet Jackson tapes, and read the autobiography of Jackie Robinson. Still, he found the United States less friendly than Italy. His new classmates were confused by the kid who spoke English with an Italian accent.

Fighting for the ball, Bryant tangles with a defender. Physical play is nothing new to Bryant. While growing up, his father would play rough with him to prepare Kobe for American basketball.

When he was fourteen, someone offered him drugs for the first time. He ran home.

He found comfort on the basketball court. It was a place where he knew he could fit in and establish himself. Kobe was an immediate sensation. His first summer at home, he joined the Sonny Hill League in Philadelphia, an elite summer camp for the area's top players. On an application, he listed pro basketball as his future occupation. A counselor who read the form scolded Kobe for having unrealistic goals.

"Don't you know that NBA players are one in a million?" the counselor asked.

"Let me tell you," Kobe said. "I'm going to be that one in a million."

He would soon be on his way.

Chapter 3

In truth, Kobe Bryant entered high school without knowing how good a player he could be. He had starred among other boys in Italy, but the competition was not very good. He could hold his own playing against his father's teammates, but what would happen when he started playing against the top American teenagers? Was his dream of making the NBA just that—a dream?

Not to worry. From the first time Kobe stepped into the Lower Merion High School gym in 1992, others could see his greatness. He was a six-foot four-inch fourteen-year-old with boundless energy and terrific talent.

"He has the potential to be something special," said varsity basketball coach Greg Downer. "He has the ability to do everything well. And he has phenomenal range on his jumper. This is a once-in-a-lifetime opportunity for me to coach a player of this caliber."

Kobe's two older sisters, Sharia and Shaya, were already starring for the Lower Merion Aces girls' basketball team. In fact, Shaya, at five feet ten inches, could already dunk the ball.

When Kobe Bryant began playing high school basketball, coaches and fans noticed his high energy level. He has brought that energetic style with him to the NBA.

Coach Downer planned to slowly work his magnificent freshman into the lineup. He did not want to put too much pressure on his youngest player. But Kobe's great talent made it seem silly to put him on the bench. He averaged 18 points per game that season, playing mostly against boys two to three years older.

Kobe also brought a quick smile to the game. His enthusiasm would become his trademark in the NBA. It was easy to spot as a teenager. His philosophy, he told everyone, was to play hard and have fun. He learned that, he said, watching his father play. After all, why play the game if you didn't enjoy it? "Dad would always have a smile going, be very calm, but be emotional," Kobe said. "That's what I would like to be. You go out there, give 100 percent and have fun."

As a sophomore, Kobe averaged 22 points and 10 rebounds per game. The Aces won 16 games and lost just 6. The season's highlight for Bryant was scoring 35 points in a playoff game against the Pennsbury High Falcons. Afterward, Pennsbury coach Brad Sharp called Kobe the best sophomore he had seen in twenty-one years of coaching.

Some people who are blessed with such talent let themselves cruise. Because they can dominate at a certain level, they do not always see the need to work hard to improve their skills. The problem is that, sooner or later, the competition gets tougher. Those who get by on talent alone eventually run across people with as much skill and more desire than they.

Kobe vowed not to let that happen. He worked out every day to keep his body strong. He also studied hard to keep his grades up. During the summer, most high school players like to stay sharp by joining a summer league. Kobe joined six of them, staying on the court from 9 A.M. to 10 P.M. Lower Merion High also did its part to keep testing Kobe. Before Kobe's junior season, Coach Downer beefed up the schedule.

He added games against the toughest high school teams in New Jersey and Pennsylvania.

"Kobe is always the first guy at the gym and the last guy out of the gym," Coach Downer said. "He has the God-given ability. But the thing that makes him special is his work ethic."

By his junior year, Kobe was six foot six and the top high school player within a hundred miles. For every game he played, the gym was full. Fans—even those of other teams—came to see the teenager who might just make it in the NBA some day. College scouts, too, packed the house. Recruiters from hundreds of schools tried to get in touch with Kobe. They wanted him to come and star for their college in another two years. The Bryant's family policy was simple: No recruiter could talk to Kobe. They could talk to Joe Bryant only.

Still, the scouts were wowed by what they saw. College coaches such as Kentucky's Rick Pitino and Duke's Mike Krzyzewski sat in the Lower Merion gym, watching with the school's student body. They saw an athletic, skillful, intelligent player. Some projected Kobe as a future Grant Hill or Anfernee Hardaway. He averaged 31 points, 10.4 rebounds, and 5.2 assists per game in his third high school season. The Aces finished 26–5, losing in the state championship tournament to Hazleton High School.

Sometimes, fans of other schools would try to throw Kobe off his game. In one game, for instance, students at Marple-Newtown High chanted, "Overrated," every time he dribbled the ball up-court. At first, Kobe was rattled. He missed six of his first eight shots. But he calmed down and made his next seven shots. On one play, he dribbled between his legs, outran three defenders, and finished with a thunderous dunk. As Marple-Newtown passed the ball back in, Kobe stole it and spun to amaze the crowd with a reverse dunk. He finished the game with a career-high 42 points.

"I don't have the words to describe him," said Marple-Newtown's Frank Zanin, who had become friends with Kobe when they played summer ball together. "We tried to go man to man all night. He's too talented. He has too many moves. When you guard him, you wish you had 20 fouls to give."

The summer before his final high school year, Kobe was invited to play in several pickup games with players on the Philadelphia 76ers. It was a big thrill to mingle with NBA players. Sixers forward Sharone Wright let Kobe, then seventeen, drive his Land Cruiser. Center Shawn Bradley would drive him home from games. Much to everyone's surprise, Kobe was able to hold his own against the pros—and sometimes beat them.

That started the talk. Would Kobe skip college and go pro? Or would he make one of the countless college coaches chasing him feel like a million-dollar lottery winner?

Kobe was not talking about it much. But he was thinking. Only a handful of players had ever tried to make the NBA straight from high school. All of them were big men with far larger and stronger bodies than Kobe Bryant's. Some of them had skipped college mostly because of poor high school grades. But Kobe was a B plus student with good scores on the college entrance tests.

What would he do? That was the big question going into Kobe's senior season. What was not in question was his status as the top high school player in the country. Kobe's final year in high school looked like a highlight film.

In December, he scored his 2,000th career point against the nation's top-ranked team, St. Anthony's High from Jersey City, New Jersey. Lower Merion lost 62–47, but Kobe led all scorers with 25.

In February, Kobe took his final bow in the Lower Merion gym. He scored 50 points against Academy Park High. He

Before Bryant's senior year of high school, he began thinking about skipping college to play in the NBA. Bryant, however, was much smaller than the other players who had successfully made that jump.

opened the game by hitting a three pointer, a driving floater, banging home a rebound, and stabbing a jumper. Add in a foul shot, and the early score was Kobe 10–Everyone Else 0.

In March 1996, the Aces beat Erie Catholic Prep for the Pennsylvania High School Championship. Erie's strategy going into the game was to stall on offense and triple-team Kobe on defense. At first it worked. Kobe was held scoreless in the first quarter. And with less than four minutes left in the game, Lower Merion trailed, 41–39. Kobe tied the score with two foul shots. Then he stole the ball and nailed a three pointer. In the end, the Aces won, 48–43.

It was Kobe's final high school game. He got to snip down the nets, as champions always do. He stood on the winner's platform with a gold medal around his neck. A reporter, wondering if Kobe had decided between college and the pros, asked, "What are you going to do now?"

"I'm going to take a shower and get dressed," Kobe said, evading the question. "And I'm going to party."

And party he did. Kobe did not have a regular girlfriend, so when the Lower Merion High School prom came up in May, he had to find a date. He invited Brandy, a teenage singing sensation and star of the situation comedy *Moesha*. They had met once, at a basketball camp, and had become long-distance telephone friends. Brandy arrived from Los Angeles with her mother, as well as a bodyguard, hairdresser, and fashion coordinator. Instead of a parent's snapshots, the couple had their pictures taken by *People* magazine. Other students asked them for their autographs.

Kobe's high school numbers were phenomenal. As a senior, he averaged 31 points per game, along with 12 rebounds, 6.5 assists, 4 steals, and 3.8 blocked shots. He was named to the McDonald's All-American team. He won a stack of national high school player-of-the-year awards. During his

Some felt that Bryant would make a mistake by not playing college basketball.

four years at Lower Merion, he scored 2,883 points, the most in Pennsylvania history.

Now he had to decide. Kobe and his parents had narrowed down the choice of colleges he might attend to a handful. Tops on the list was Philadelphia's LaSalle University, where Joe Bryant worked as an assistant coach. It was not a glamorous program, but it was a chance to stay home and play for his dad. Also on the list were national powerhouses such as Duke, Kentucky, Michigan, and North Carolina. Any of them could provide a great experience.

But, of course, skipping college entirely was another choice. Some experts said he would make a mistake by jumping straight to the NBA. Others thought he could be a star within a season or two.

Newspapers and talk shows buzzed with the question in the spring of 1996. What would Kobe do? Even his friends were asked for their opinion. It is probably smarter for him to go to college, said classmate Charity Brown. But it is cooler to go to the NBA.

Ultimately, only Kobe could make the decision.

Chapter 4

The Lower Merion High School gym was packed on April 29, 1996. Students jostled for space with reporters from big-city newspapers and ESPN. The school's teachers stood by watching. Members of the local singing group, Boyz II Men, came to watch their friend and main man, Kobe Bryant.

At 2:30 P.M., Kobe walked up to a microphone, lifted up his sunglasses, and announced his decision.

"I've decided to skip college and take my talents to the NBA," he said. "I'm a person who loves competitiveness. I want to go out there and do the best I can with the best competition."

His classmates cheered wildly. Many of the teachers shook their heads in disapproval. They had wanted Kobe to pursue his education in college. Kobe's parents stood by him in support. Overall, the reaction was very mixed.

Even Coach Downer, one of Kobe's biggest supporters, had mixed feelings. "I'm worried about whether he can hold up physically," the coach said. "And I don't want such a good person to fall into the traps and evils of the NBA. I want this to have a very rosy ending. I think it can. But danger lurks out there."

How much danger? That was a matter of opinion. Some people felt that Kobe's biggest problem would be adjusting to adult life at age seventeen. Professional sports may seem like a glamorous career, but it is a grueling lifestyle of traveling from city to city, living in hotels, and dealing with temptations. Kobe had never even lived away from home before.

Kobe's parents understood that challenge. They said they would move to whatever city Kobe went to as a pro. Perhaps they would even travel with the team. Kobe would not be without family when starting his career.

Beyond that was the question of whether he was yet good enough to compete in the NBA. Being the country's top high school player was one thing. Trying to stop Michael Jordan, Allen Iverson, and Grant Hill was quite another.

Until 1974, the NBA had an age rule that kept players out of the league until their college class graduated. But a court decided that rule was illegal. If a player was good enough, the court said, his age should not matter.

Since then, just six players had ever tried jumping to the NBA straight from high school. Two ended up being busts. A third, Darryl Dawkins, had some success, although experts said he would have had a better career if he had some college training.

That left Moses Malone, Shawn Kemp, and Kevin Garnett.

Moses Malone joined the old American Basketball Association (ABA) straight from high school in 1974. Over the next two decades, he set rebounding records and won an NBA title with the Philadelphia 76ers. Shawn Kemp enrolled in junior college, but never played, before joining the Seattle SuperSonics in 1989. He became a yearly choice for the All-Star team. And, one year before Kobe, Chicago high school star Kevin Garnett

On April 29, 1996, Kobe Bryant made the announcement that he would enter the upcoming NBA draft.

went right to the Minnesota Timberwolves. Within a season or two, he was regarded as a rising star.

Those three men, however, were big-bodied men who relied on size as much as skill. Kobe, even at six-foot-seven, would be almost frail by NBA standards. It is tougher for a guard than a big man to break into the big leagues. The position usually requires more experience. And whether Kobe would be an NBA shooter remained unclear.

"This kid is making a catastrophic mistake," warned NBA scouting director Marty Blake. "Kevin Garnett was the best high school player I ever saw, and I wouldn't have advised him to jump to the NBA. And Kobe is no Kevin Garnett."

Maybe so, but most NBA insiders believed that Kobe would be among the first twelve or fifteen players taken in the league's draft of incoming players. That would likely get him a three-year contract worth about $3.5 million.

In fact, Kobe started earning riches even before the draft. In May 1996, the Adidas footwear company signed him to a five hundred thousand dollar deal to promote its sneakers. He used the money to buy himself a sport utility vehicle. He also bought his two sisters some jewelry and some new dresses. The Adidas campaign featured him as "a kid with a dream." Kobe's dream? To make the last-second winning basket in the NBA championship game.

But for which team? Being from the East coast, Kobe told everyone he would not mind playing for the New York Knicks, New Jersey Nets, or Philadelphia 76ers. His first choice, though, was the Los Angeles Lakers. Do not forget, as a little boy he loved wearing his Lakers jacket. His favorite player was always Lakers star guard Magic Johnson.

Of course, amateur players have no say on which team gets them. The NBA draft runs from worst team to best, so that the teams with the poorest records one season get first crack at the best new players in the next season. Whichever of the twenty-nine NBA teams wanted Kobe had the right to take him.

The draft was held on June 26, 1996. The 76ers chose first, and picked speedy guard Allen Iverson from Georgetown University. Other big-time college stars, such as Marcus Camby of Massachusetts and Stephon Marbury of Georgia Tech, were early picks. Then, with the thirteenth pick of the first round, the Charlotte Hornets selected Kobe Bryant of Lower Merion High School.

The pick surprised Kobe. Many teams had spoken with him before the draft. The Hornets were not among them. He was not happy, but he did not want to show it.

"I've been to Italy," he said. "I've been to Spain. But I've never been to Charlotte. But I'm in the NBA. It feels like heaven. This is what I've been waiting for all my life."

Immediately, rumors swirled that the Hornets had drafted Kobe just to trade him. Hornets general manager Dave Cowens dismissed Kobe as a child who would have a tough time breaking into the league. Kobe was a bit hurt. If Charlotte did not want him, he thought to himself, he did not want Charlotte.

A few days later, the rumored trade was made. The Hornets sent Kobe to the Lakers in exchange for center Vlade Divac. Then, just a few days later, the Lakers added to their talent by signing free-agent center Shaquille O'Neal away from the Orlando Magic.

Kobe's dream had come true. He had the chance to play with the team he grew up loving. On July 12, 1996, he was introduced to Los Angeles fans by Lakers general manager Jerry West, who handed Kobe a gold-and-purple jersey with the number eight.

What would the Lakers do with an eighteen-year-old phenom? Lakers coach Del Harris would not say what position he

Bryant was originally drafted by the Charlotte Hornets. A few days later, Charlotte traded his rights to the Los Angeles Lakers in exchange for center Vlade Divac.

wanted Bryant to play. But he compared Bryant's playing style with that of Lakers swingman Eddie Jones. West said he did not expect Bryant to be an immediate NBA star. Instead, West said, Bryant would become a player that fans would talk about for more than a decade.

Suddenly, a new life was beginning for the Bryant family. The entire clan—both parents and both sisters—joined Kobe in moving west. They bought a house near Los Angeles in Pacific Palisades. It has six bedrooms, six bathrooms, a Jacuzzi, Italian-marble floors, and a view of the Pacific Ocean. The neighbors include actors Arnold Schwarzenegger and Tom Cruise.

Kobe Bryant said it was important to him that the family stay together. He might be old enough to play in the pros, he said, but that did not make him too old to take advice from his parents. "Other kids don't have a father," he said. "I don't have anything in common with them. My father is my best friend."

Kobe Bryant's family would help him with his personal life. Professionally, however, he had to do it himself. Bryant hired a personal trainer. He joined a gym in Venice Beach and went five times a week to wrestle with the workout machines. He added muscles to his body and a goatee to his chin. Even so, he was the skinniest, youngest-looking player in the Lakers training camp.

The team Bryant was joining was already one of the best in the NBA. The Lakers won 53 games in 1995–96, and lost just 29. They were led that season by forward Cedric Ceballos, who averaged 21 points per game. Point guard Nick Van Exel averaged 15 points and nearly seven assists per game. And, remarkably, Magic Johnson unretired after four full seasons out of the game to join the team for thirty-two games at midseason.

Still, something was wrong with the chemistry. The Lakers were knocked out of the NBA playoffs in the first round. They

Kobe Bryant would be joining an exciting Lakers team that featured guard Eddie
Jones and All-Star center Shaquille O'Neal.

had a lot of good players. But the players did not seem to fit together as a group. So changes were made. Ceballos was traded, along with several other starters. Shaquille O'Neal, one of the NBA's top scorers and rebounders, was brought in to lead the club. Eddie Jones was expected to take a larger role in the 1996–97 season.

Into this group came Kobe Bryant. Coach Harris did not expect Bryant to make a dramatic impact as an eighteen-year-old rookie. Kobe Bryant, however, had different expectations.

Chapter 5

Everyone faces doubters at some point in his or her life. Everyone is told that his goal is not achievable. Everyone hears the words, "Give it up."

Some give it up. It is easier, at times, to quit. But others hear the critics and the doubters and decide to work twice as hard at getting to their goal. Those people are the true winners.

Kobe Bryant had more than his share of critics when he joined the NBA in 1996. At age eighteen, he was the youngest player in the league's history.

Who was this boy who was daring enough to play against the best male basketball players in the world? Sure, he had grown to six feet seven inches, but he barely weighed two hundred pounds. Could he take the pounding of bumping up against NBA giants such as Patrick Ewing and Hakeem Olajuwon?

And, while everyone praised Bryant for his smarts, he was, after all, still a teenager. There were lessons to be learned, and court-savvy veterans such as Michael Jordan and John Stockton would surely show no mercy on the inexperienced youngster.

Many experts expected Bryant to fail—and told him so. Even the men who ran the Lakers were not quite sure what to expect. What concerned them the most was how their child-among-men would adjust to the grueling lifestyle of pro basketball. Remember, by skipping college, Bryant skipped the transition between high school and the NBA. In high school, he played thirty games a season. He got to the game in his dad's car, and slept in his bedroom afterward. Now, he would be playing up to a hundred games a season, flying around the country, and sleeping in different hotels every night.

"When Kobe came onto the team, we said, 'Oh my gosh, what are we going to have to do extra for this kid? How are we going to watch over him?'" said Lakers general manager Jerry West. "But we haven't had to do anything. He's mature beyond his years." It helped, of course, that Bryant's entire family had moved out with him from Philadelphia.

Bryant was lucky enough to have two other men who took on the role of mentor. A mentor is an experienced person who takes on the role of tutor or trusted counselor.

The first mentor was Magic Johnson, the Lakers great point guard. Remember, when Bryant was growing up in Italy, he spent endless hours watching Johnson highlights on video. A Magic Johnson poster hung on his wall. After being traded to the Lakers, his first call was to Magic, asking, "Can we work out together?"

Johnson had retired, tried a comeback, and retired again just before Bryant joined the team. He looked at this brash, bold youngster, and saw himself twenty years earlier. Magic promised to take care of Bryant, but he said he would also criticize him when the need arose. He said Bryant needed to—and would—learn to read the game, to let it flow through him. And he warned everyone to be patient with the teenager.

Kobe Bryant's other mentor was Lakers center Shaquille

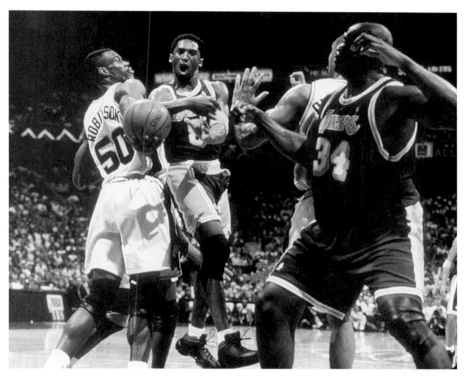

Weaving his way through traffic, Kobe Bryant slips a pass to teammate Shaquille O'Neal.

O'Neal, who took on the role of big brother. O'Neal is one of the flashiest players in the NBA. But, in Bryant, he saw someone who might be flashier. He gave Bryant the nickname Showboat. One time, in training camp, O'Neal bet Bryant on how high he could jump. Bryant touched the top of the backboard square. O'Neal said it was like watching a coiled spring release.

In practices, O'Neal and Bryant quickly developed an on-court chemistry. But who knew what to expect when the real games began?

Bryant's second pro game was back home, in Philadelphia, against the Philadelphia 76ers. His hometown friends and family packed the CoreStates Center and gave him the loudest ovation during introductions.

Bryant played in parts of the second and third quarters and looked as if he belonged on the court with the grown men. He flipped a pass behind his back to O'Neal, who slammed it home for two points. Bryant led a fast break, missed the layup, but got his own rebound and dunked the ball behind his head to shouts of "Ko-be!" Later, he stole a pass and raced alone to the basket. He slowed at the foul line and looked over his shoulder at the trailing defender as if to taunt him. Bryant dunked the ball with a little hang onto the rim for good measure.

The play angered the Sixers. They saw it as arrogant, especially for an eighteen year old playing just his second game. A few minutes later, Bryant took a pass in the corner. He drove the baseline. As he began to leap for another dunk, he was slammed to the floor by 76ers center Scott Williams. He lay there, not moving. The crowd gasped. Bryant finally got up, but he had hurt his wrist. He sat out the rest of the game, but he had learned a lesson.

"I told him after the game, the more you embarrass the big guys by dunking the ball, the more they come after you and foul you hard," said Lakers teammate Eddie Jones. "I think he won't do it again."

There were other lessons to be learned. In high school, Bryant was expected to shoot the ball most times he touched it. But not on the Lakers. Here he was surrounded by talented teammates such as O'Neal and Jones. His instructions from Coach Del Harris were to think of passing first and shoot only if he had the perfect shot. Sometimes Bryant listened. Sometimes he could not contain himself. He was fighting between his instincts and what his coach told him.

"He may see me as the first adult who told him he was wrong," said Coach Harris. "I don't want to be remembered as the guy who wouldn't let Kobe Bryant play. But I have to do that. I can't give him special treatment just because he's eighteen."

Through the first half of his rookie season, Bryant was averaging just eleven minutes a game—less than a quarter. Sometimes he looked great, sometimes he looked awful. In one home game against the Chicago Bulls, Bryant outleaped Michael Jordan and blocked a shot by "His Airness." It was highlight film stuff, and the Lakers won the game by sixteen. On the other hand, Jordan outscored Bryant 27 to 5 that night. Bryant made just two of seven shots.

Around the league, though, fans seemed to love the teenaged wonder. And he loved the fans, especially at Los Angeles' Great Western Forum. Jack Nicholson was the most prominent of the $1,000-a-game courtside celebrities. Sometimes Jerry Seinfeld stopped by, sometimes Tiger Woods. The retired jerseys of Lakers greats Elgin Baylor, Jerry West, Wilt Chamberlain, Magic Johnson, and Kareem Abdul-Jabbar all hung from the rafters. Some day, many predicted, Bryant's number eight jersey would join them up there.

Sure he was making mistakes, but everyone saw the

Watching from the side, Kobe Bryant cheers on his teammates. During Bryant's rookie season he needed time to learn the pro game and only played 15.5 minutes per game.

potential. Once, Robert Horry, a role player on the club, was asked how Bryant was fitting in with the rest of the team. "Pretty soon other players will have to fit around him," Horry said. "Kobe's going to be the best player ever."

Better than Jordan?

"Yep. Kobe's got Michael's skills and Michael's will. But Kobe came into the league when he was eighteen, and he's going to be able to accomplish more."

As the season went on, Bryant's game improved. He was invited to the NBA All-Star weekend in Cleveland, where he won the NBA's Slam Dunk Contest. He played in the Rookie All-Star Game and scored an event-record 31 points.

By season's end, Bryant's play had really picked up. He averaged 11.4 points per game in the final thirteen contests. His best game was a 24-point, 9-for-11 shooting night in a 109–85 win at Golden State on April 8. He ranked third on the team with a .819 free-throw percentage.

He played in seventy-one games during the 1996–97 season, as a shooting guard, point guard, and small forward. He averaged 7.6 points, 1.9 rebounds, and 1.3 assists per game. They were not great numbers, but nothing to be ashamed of either. He never looked overmatched, just inexperienced.

"What Kobe is, is a bundle of energy," said Coach Harris. "But you can't have one hit song and be compared with Frank Sinatra. Greatness comes with consistency over time."

The season ended on a sour note, both for Bryant and the Lakers. The team was knocked out of the NBA playoffs in five games by the Utah Jazz. In the final game in Salt Lake City, Bryant threw up three air balls, all in overtime. If he had made any one of them, the Lakers might have had a victory.

After that loss, the Lakers flight touched down in Los Angeles at 2 A.M. Bryant went home to bed. Four hours later

One highlight of Bryant's rookie season was winning the Slam Dunk Competition during the 1997 All-Star Weekend.

he got up, drove to a high school gym, and took shot after shot for the next three hours.

Was he punishing himself?

"Not at all," he said. "I was just playing ball. That's what I love to do. It was fun."

Maybe so. But no one failed to notice that most of Bryant's shots that morning came from the exact spot on the court where he had missed the final shot the night before. One night's failure was not going to stop Kobe Bryant. If hard work and constant practice was the way to reach his goal, he would not mind sweating by himself in a high school gym at 6 A.M.

Chapter 6

What separates the good athletes from the great, once-in-a-generation immortals? First off, there is talent. Health and durability play roles, too. Luck can be a factor, because a great athlete on a bad team may not get his or her chance to shine.

One other key is an athlete's sheer desire. Every pro team has some players who are just happy to be on the roster or to be a starter. But there are a select few who are never satisfied. This handful—like Michael Jordan, Steve Young, or Mark Messier—have a boundless need. It is not money that satisfies them; it is stardom and championships. They are all about ambition.

When experts and teammates predict that Kobe Bryant will some day be the top star in the NBA, they are not just looking at his talent. They also see his drive, his hunger, and his on-court nasty streak. Like Jordan, Bryant is not beyond trash talk or a well-placed elbow.

"Why would you even play if you didn't want to be the best player who ever lived?" Bryant has asked. "That's how I would think everyone would go into it. You want to be the man. Not just the best of the moment, but the best who ever set foot on the basketball court."

That is why, after the disappointing end to his rookie season, Bryant got up the next morning at six o'clock and took shots in a high school gym. It is why, that summer, he worked out seven days a week with personal trainer Joe Carbone. The two men would start the morning with a three-mile run. Then they would work out at a gym for an hour. Then they would head to a court for two hours of shooting. In the late afternoon, Bryant would head to the UCLA college campus, where he would join in pickup games between NBA players and top college stars. Not once that summer did he take a day off.

Now, at night, he lies in bed and watches videotapes of the Lakers playing. It is just what he did as a child over in Italy. But now, instead of watching Magic Johnson play, he watches himself. It is almost as if he imagined his future so hard that he made it come true. So he studies himself on the court, looking to see if he should have passed instead of shot, or maybe rotated defensively.

When the 1997–98 season began, Bryant was still the NBA's youngest player. But he was no longer the most inexperienced. Quickly, he served notice of how much he had improved.

Early in the season, the Lakers played against the Chicago Bulls and Bryant's other hero, Michael Jordan. As the Lakers sixth man, Bryant did not even start, but came off the bench roughly seven minutes into the game. The first two times he got the ball, he passed, just as Coach Del Harris wanted him to. Then, the third time up the court, he took a long pass from teammate Nick Van Exel in the corner. Bryant faked a shot, then ducked under Bulls forward Scottie Pippen, who had gone for the fake. He threw up a shot almost from his knees. It swished through the net for two points.

Many observers were surprised to see the amount of improvement Bryant made between his first and second years in the league.

Bryant made his next shot, and then the one after that. He blocked a three-point try by Bulls guard Steve Kerr and dribbled down the court all alone. As fans roared and cameras clicked, Bryant stuffed home a reverse jam that made that night's highlight shows. He ran past cheering fans, holding his arms up as if to say, "Sometimes I amaze myself."

He scored a career-high 33 points that night. It was four more than the great Jordan.

The 1997–98 Lakers were a young team, with all of their players under thirty. Sometimes they looked like a championship club. Other times they looked confused and inexperienced. Still, at midseason, they were 39–17, second to the Seattle SuperSonics in the Pacific Division. They sent four players to the NBA All-Star Game—center Shaquille O'Neal, and guards Eddie Jones, Nick Van Exel, and Kobe Bryant.

Some thought it was more than Bryant deserved. After all, how many players make it to the All-Star Game who do not even start for their team? Critics shook their heads when they saw the NBA's newspaper ads promoting the game. On one side of the full-page ad was a picture of Jordan. On the other side was Kobe Bryant. His tongue was dangling, just like that of the NBA king.

Did Kobe Bryant belong? Of course he did, and the fans at New York City's Madison Square Garden quickly saw why. The youngest all-star in NBA history led his team with 18 points and 6 rebounds. In the game's most exciting play, he waved off teammates so that he could go one-on-one against Jordan. Bryant faked right, and when Jordan went for the move, Bryant breezed toward the basket for a layup.

Most of the league's older stars were impressed with this young phenomenon. A handful, most notably Utah Jazz star Karl Malone, accused him of hogging the ball. "When a younger guy tells me to get out of the way, that's a game I don't need to be in." said Malone.

Jordan, who had been labeled a ball hog early in his career, knew what Bryant was going through. After the game, Jordan ushered the nineteen-year-old aside in a Madison Square Garden corner for a brief moment of superstar advice.

"I just hugged him and told him to keep going and stay strong because there are always expectations," Jordan said afterward. "I know what too much pressure can do to you. I just wanted him to be aware. He's a smart kid with a bright future. He'll figure it out."

The stats for Bryant's second pro season show that he is figuring it out. He played in 79 games, all but one as a reserve. He averaged 15.4 points per game, along with 3.1 rebounds, and 2.5 assists. His shooting percentage was fairly low—just .428—but he showed he was learning when to pass and when to shoot.

The Lakers finished the season with 61 wins and just 21 losses. In the first two rounds of the playoffs, they blew away the Portland Trail Blazers and the Seattle SuperSonics. The highlight for Bryant was the series-clinching 110–99 win over Portland. He scored 22 points. His best play came when he picked the pocket of Portland forward Cliff Robinson, streaked down the floor, and unleashed a three pointer that hit nothing but net.

Eventually, the Lakers were swept away, four games to none, by the Utah Jazz in the 1998 Western Conference Finals. But it had been a fine season for the team. And with a young nucleus of Bryant, and Shaquille O'Neal, Los Angeles fans felt they would have a winning club for years to come.

Soon after the season ended, Bryant was asked how disappointed he felt about getting swept by the Jazz in the playoffs.

"I know it sounds strange," he said, "but the way the season

Knifing toward the basket, Bryant tries to lay a finger roll past the outstretched arms of Trail Blazers forward Brian Grant.

ended was exactly what I needed to get ready for the next season. It ended with me having to take a long look at my game and what I need to do to improve it."

That is what Kobe Bryant is all about. He is confident, but not afraid to look at his faults and try to improve them. He knows how to have fun, but he also has the work ethic that is needed by anyone who wants to be the best.

Bryant's hero and role model, Magic Johnson, has said, "See, the kids in America, they don't do the work that Kobe does. That's a problem with the young people now. They don't have the fundamentals."

Bryant continued to work on his fundamentals in 1999. He averaged just a tick under 20 points per game to rank fifteenth in the NBA. He set career personal highs for rebounds, assists, steals, and shooting percentage. He was named to the 1999 All-NBA third team. And remember, he was not even twenty-one years old yet.

In one memorable game against the Orlando Magic, Bryant scored just 5 points in the first half. His shooting touch was definitely off. At halftime, as his teammates rested, Bryant snuck off into a private room next to the Lakers locker room. By himself—and without a basketball—he practiced taking jump shots. Again and again, he lifted off the ground and flicked his wrists. As Magic Johnson would say, he was working on the fundamentals.

His work paid off. Bryant was on fire in the second half. He hit 13 of 15 shots, nearly all of them jumpers. Even his own teammates watched in awe as he nailed swish after swish. In all, he scored 33 second-half points. The Lakers came from behind to beat the Magic.

Many fans and even players talk about Bryant's similarities to Michael Jordan. He jumps like Jordan. He slashes and creates his own shots, much like Jordan. In those times when

Sean Elliot of the San Antonio Spurs can only watch as Kobe Bryant is about to complete a reverse jam.

Bryant needs the extra split second to air his shot, he can hang in the air, just like the gravity-defying Chicago Bulls legend. He even sounds like Jordan when answering reporters' questions. That comes from studying Jordan on tape.

In fact, every once in a while, Bryant's teammates turn around the Jordan-Bryant comparison.

"Sometimes you say Michael could do things Kobe does," Lakers guard Jon Barry said. "And sometimes it's unanimous he couldn't."

Like Jordan did, Bryant works out every day with a personal trainer. On game days, early in the morning, he meets his trainer at the gym. They lift weights and stretch before Bryant meets his teammates for a shoot-around.

Working out is one thing. Working on his team game is another. The biggest knock on Bryant has been his desire to shoot rather than pass. But that was the same thing that was said about Jordan during his first seven years in the NBA. Only after the Bulls won their first NBA title in 1991 was Jordan considered a great player who could elevate his teammates, much like Magic Johnson and Larry Bird.

The Lakers are not yet built around Kobe Bryant. Some day they probably will be, along with center Shaquille O'Neal. "When you look at the NBA champions, most of them had a one-two punch," said O'Neal. He imagines himself and Bryant as that combination.

At nineteen, Bryant was already the Lakers' best one-on-one player. His ability to create his own shot, as well as dish off to his teammates, will be crucial to the team's success. Certainly, he has much to learn. But with his talent, instincts, and tremendous work ethic, he has a great chance to become a superb player who leads his teammates to a title.

Career Statistics

YEAR	TEAM	GP	FG%	REB	AST	STL	BLK	PTS	AVG
1996–97	Lakers	71	.417	132	91	49	23	539	7.6
1997–98	Lakers	79	.428	242	199	74	40	1,220	15.4
1998–99	Lakers	50	.465	264	190	72	50	996	19.9
Totals		200	.439	638	480	195	113	2,755	13.8

GP=Games Played   REB=Rebounds   STL=Steals   PTS=Points
FG%=Field Goal Percentage   AST=Assists   BLK=Blocks   AVG=Average

Where to Write Kobe Bryant:

Mr. Kobe Bryant
c/o Los Angeles Lakers
Great Western Forum
3900 W. Manchester Blvd.
Inglewood, CA 90305

On the Internet at:

http://www.nba.com/playerfile/kobe_bryant.html
http://www.nba.com/Lakers

Index